Leaving Time: A Novel by Jodi Picoult - Reviewed

By
J.T. Salrich

J.T. Salrich

CONTENTS

J.T. Salrich

About the author

Jodi Lynn Picoult was born May 19, 1966 in Nesconset, New York. She is an American author who was awarded the New England Bookseller Award for fiction in 2003. Picoult currently has approximately 14 million copies of her books in print worldwide. She studied writing at Princeton University ('87) and earned a master's degree in education from Harvard University.

She wrote five issues of the Wonder Woman comic book series for DC Comics. Her 23 novels are translated into thirty four languages in thirty five countries. Four – *The Pact, Plain Truth, The Tenth Circle, and Salem Falls* - have been made into television movies. *My Sister's Keeper* was a big-screen released from New Line Cinema, with Nick Cassavetes directing and Cameron Diaz starring, which is now available in DVD.

Jodi is part of the Writer's Council for the National Writing Project, which recognizes the universality of writing as a communicative tool and helps teachers enhance student writing. She is a spokesperson for Positive Tracks/Children's Hospital at Dartmouth, which supports youth-led charity fundraising through athletics; and is on the advisory committee of the New Hampshire Coalition against the Death Penalty. She is also the founder and executive producer of the Trumbull Hall Troupe, a New Hampshire-based teen theater group that performs original musicals to raise money for local charities; to date their contributions have exceeded $100K.

She and her husband Tim and their three children live in Hanover, New Hampshire with two Springer spaniels, two rescue puppies, two donkeys, two geese, ten chickens, a smattering of ducks, and the occasional Holstein.

Themes

Self-preservation and the fear of abandonment persists throughout which causes characters to make decisions that ultimately hides or denies the truth. Well-intentioned characters who try to help or protect others becomes the shield they hide behind.

Symbols

Elephants are the dominant symbols throughout the book, representing wisdom, fertility, and female matriarchies. Reality and the imagined are brought into account through the use of characters developed both in the ghost/spirit realm and the human realm. Deciphering which is which is left to the reader to determine.

Settings

The majority of this story takes place at the New England Elephant Sanctuary in New Hampshire, the Botswana game reserve, Phalaborwa, South Africa, and the Tennessee Elephant Sanctuary. All are places where joy and grief, spiritual development, and maturity occur.

Short Summary

Leaving Time weaves elephant behavior into a search for a missing mother and focuses on motherhood, loss, and grief. Teenager Jenna Metcalf was just three years old when her mother disappeared from an elephant sanctuary. Ten years later, she takes up the search for her mother, Alice, by studying Alice's decade-old journals on grieving elephants. The research itself is fascinating, but Jenna cannot find her mother on her own. By enlisting the help of a formerly famous psychic and the private detective whose career went south during the botched investigation of Alice's disappearance, Jenna forms a team to help her in her quest.

Prologue-Jenna

Jenna, the presumed main character, begins her narration by considering myths versus truths, fact and fiction. She explains her mother's beliefs that rational, scientific thought can explain reality. She appears to be reminiscing about her mother, but it is unclear what has happened. The scene is set in Jenna's mind and her memories.

Analysis

Picoult's introduction of Jenna, the daughter of a scientist, piques an interest as to the clash between myth development and scientific explanation. Science is based on data and data analysis that presumably logically analyzes an argument, theory, or hypothesis. Myths involve supernatural beings, which are necessarily beyond rational, scientific thought.

Study Questions

Why does Picoult introduce *Leaving Time* with a myth buster?

What significance do myths have when juxtaposed with scientific explanations?

Does one point to reality better than the other?

Important Terms

Elephant Graveyard
Mass burial site
Myths

Quotations

"Jenna, she would have told me, there's an explanation for everything you see."

Prologue-Alice

This chapter introduces another daughter, Jenna's mom. Alice recounts the story of her becoming a scientist and her love of and passion for the plight of African elephants. She recalls the emotional childhood moments that lead her to become the voice for elephants. Through witnessing the lack of space and freedom that a zoo elephant had, she becomes sensitive to its suffering and the suffering of elephants in general. Her narration describes her love of factual data, but she describes her anger and intuitive responses as critical components that motivate her to become a scientist.

Analysis

Alice's first-person narration is told as if she is still alive, making a reader wonder why Jenna reminisces about her. Alice reminisces about an innocent child's perspective on making a difference in life. She describes her considerable effort as a 9-year old little girl to help the zoo elephant seem like a failure that amounted to nothing. Yet, she receives community acknowledgement and encouragement in the form of an award and an article in *The Boston Globe*. She introduces the human-like characteristics of an elephant's personality, a suggestion that she may consider them to be her friends.

Study Questions

How does Alice's memory of her mother compare to Jenna's recounting of Alice?

Why is Alice able to sympathize with an elephant's suffering? What can or does she learn from their suffering? How does it lead her to change her behavior?

Important Terms

Indian Sari
Special Concerned Citizen Award
Elephant Advocate
Sieve

Quotations

"Elephants are as unique in their personalities as humans are, and just as you would not assume that two random humans would become close friends, you should not assume that two elephants will bond simply because they are both elephants."

"...like trying to stem the tide with a sieve."

"The moral of this story is that no matter how much we try, no matter how much we want it ... some stories just don't have a happy ending."

Part 1
Chapter One-Jenna

Picoult begins the chapter with a poem called *The Elephant*. The poem is told using the voice and perspective of an elephant who is self-reflecting. It describes how it self-perceives as a "man of self-cultivation" and discusses how it is misperceived by people as humble.

Jenna continues to reminisce about her mother and recalls a memory at the age of 9 months of her mother's sweetness. As a thirteen year old, her interest in memory studies mark her as mature for her age. She, too, enjoys scientific facts like her mother, but acknowledges that she *fails miserably* with real-life facts.

We learn for the first time about Jenna's parents. First, we learn that Alice has disappeared. Jenna relates the details of the events in a matter-of-fact way by listing what she currently knows of the disappearance. On the other hand, Jenna's father is psychiatrically institutionalized. She is wholly unable to relate to him, though forced by her grandmother to interact with him. Overall, we are left with an impression that Jenna is consumed with the memory and disappearance of her mother and has no relationship with her father that she can speak of.

Jenna takes it upon herself to investigate her mom's disappearance, but when she finds very little, she succumbs to her intuition and speaks with a pink-haired psychic named Serenity. After much debate and argument, the psychic eventually gives Jenna a nugget of information that changes her entire investigative strategy: her mother is still alive.

Analysis
Jenna's insight and intelligence suggest she is a gifted child who, at the age of thirteen, probably knows more than her teachers. She, however, has trouble making friends, alluding to the idea that Alice posed about elephants: just because you put humans together doesn't mean that they will get along. Jenna's view of her mother and grandmother as strong-minded, intelligent female leaders flies in direct contrast to her view of her dad as an unavailable person wholly unable to care for himself. In addition to abandonment, this weak, absent male symbol suggests an ineptitude undeserving of respect. Jenna's visit to the psychic shows a point of independence that deviates from her mother's beliefs.

Study Questions

How does Jenna's view of her mother and father shape her experience as a school-aged girl?

Is she becoming her mother?

Important Terms
Heroic courtesy
Memory/amnesiac
Melancholy migrations
Sanctuary

Quotations

"Anyone so ceremonious suffers breakdowns."

"…that memory is linked to strong emotion, and that negative moments are like scribbling with permanent marker on the wall of the brain"

"…shivering at the thought of being so close to someone I recognized and didn't know at all…"

"Data collection is the weapon of the private investigator, and facts are your friends."

"If we are to be honest as scientists … we must admit there may be a few things that we are not supposed to know. I took that as a sign."

"Most missing people disappear because they want to," Serenity says."

Chapter Two-Alice

Alice continues to describe more about an elephant's holistic intelligence. This includes memory or recollection of past harms, most of which is primarily based on an elephant's sense of smell. Elephants know who their friends are and do not forget a past injury.

Analysis

Still unable to determine whether Alice is alive, she speaks to us as a teacher would. Alice cites several examples of how elephants can remember occurrences several decades apart and how their sense of smell can be incredibly accurate. She insinuates that their instinct is more refined than humans because they know who is trying to hurt them, as opposed to humans who continuously put themselves in harm's way. The ending seems to suggest that Alice may be learning as much about herself by studying elephants as she does about them.

Study Questions

Why does Alice find it so important to share her knowledge about elephants?

What is it about them that she is trying to get the reader to understand?

Beyond understanding that they are intelligent beings, it seems as if Alice elevates them to being superior to humans? Do you agree or disagree?

Important Terms

Mahout

Masai/Kamba

Quotations:

"[T]he question isn't whether elephants can remember. Maybe we need to ask: What won't they forget?"

Chapter Three-Serenity

This chapter introduces Serenity, the psychic that Jenna visits. Serenity begins to describe her unique ability to see spirits that are beyond most people's ability to see. Her awkward childhood and ability to predict terrified her parents to the point that they ask her to suppress her gift. She tries, but feels terrible when she's able to see people's future pain and does not say something to attempt to prevent it from occurring. Her Gift is both remarkably accurate in some instances and woefully blind in others. She could not, for example, foresee her parent's deaths nor can she predict the stock market.

It was not until college that Serenity begins to appreciate her talents through the support and friendship of Shanae. Together, they dabble in the occult and find Serenity's spirit guides, Lucinda and Desmond. Her specialty with missing children make her a favorite with police departments and the media. Serenity becomes a celebrity figure herself, but becomes obsessed with fame and glory. She humiliates herself one day on television and devastates the family of a Senator whose son has been missing. Thanks to Serenity, they find the son, but unlike her prediction that he was safe, they go to the location and only find his remains. Afterwards, Serenity is shunned by celebrities and the powerful figures who once adored her.

After meeting Jenna, Serenity has a powerful dream that allows her to see what has happened to Alice. Only the reader is made aware of this, but Serenity knows that she can help Jenna find her mom.

Analysis

Serenity's supernatural abilities almost make her other worldly, but when we learn that she cannot predict all things, her fallibility makes her more like an average person. Her wild success and subsequent downfall make her as egotistical and human as someone without the Gift. Notably, after she asks her spirit guides to go away, she is unable to use her Gift. Such an ability for her guides to give or take her Gift make it seem as if it is not hers. Without her guides, her downfall and shame consist of becoming a fake psychic just so that she can subsist. That is, until she meets her own guide, Jenna, who may yet lead her back to the Gift.

Study Questions

Why do you think Serenity refers to her psychic gifts as her second sight?

If you could predict the future, would you no longer believe that there is a point to living?

Was Serenity's gift all her own?

Important Terms

Second sight
Scrying
Swamp witch
Cold reading

Quotations
"My parents had said that, if I didn't hide my second sight, I'd get hurt. But it was better that I get hurt than someone else."
"I don't really want to see the whole landscape of the future. I mean, if I could, what's the point of living?"
"Dreaming is the closest the average human gets to the paranormal plane."

Chapter Four

Alice continues her lessons on the elephant grieving process. Elephants grieve in a way that shows reverence towards their herd and the individual elephant that has died. They have a great respect for each other and mourn the loss of an elephant in a way that acknowledges their sadness and esteem.

Analysis

We begin to understand the intricate grieving process that elephants undergo after having lost a member of the herd. Similar parallels can begin to be made between that process and Jenna's grieving process, particularly her constant return to her online Missing Persons reports and the data she has collected. Similarly, the intuition that Alice describes of elephants, is one that Jenna is beginning to cultivate in her quest to find her mother.

For the first time, we read that Alice views herself as one of the great elephant researchers. She, like the others, has documented elephant death rituals and seems to believe that this is a mark of sophisticated intelligence, both on the part of the scientist and the elephants themselves.

Study Questions:

What is it about death rituals that makes elephants intelligent?

What is it about death rituals that could make a scientist great?

Describe some parallels between an elephant's grieving process and Jenna's.

Important Terms

Death rituals

Reverence

Quotations

"For them, grief is simpler, cleaner. It's all about loss."

Chapter Five-Jenna

Here we find that Jenna has returned to Serenity's apartment to retrieve her mother's scarf. She discovers that Serenity has a dream of a woman who was hurt, but alive and breathing with an elephant surrounding her. Jenna is convinced it represents her mother, so she presses Serenity to repeat the short dream so that Jenna can scrutinize it for detail. Jenna is thrilled to have new proof and immediately wants to report it to the police. Serenity explains that it won't be that easy. But Jenna persists. She manages to convince Serenity to visit the Stark Nature Preserve, which used to be the elephant sanctuary that her dad owned and operated prior to meeting Alice.

As Jenna and Serenity walk around, strange, perhaps coincidental, events occur that lead them both to find a leather wallet that once belonged to Alice. Both are stunned. Jenna eventually returns the police station and finds more clues that lead her to the investigator who used to be on her mom's case. She eventually contacts him and begins to find new facts to decipher, including insight that she has while visiting her father.

Analysis

The discussion between Jenna and Serenity relates back to Alice's observations of one way that elephants recall events. Serenity describes a bit more about the manner she used to find missing persons. She tells Serenity that she used to hold a piece of the property that once belonged to the missing person. This would either help her see a flash of an image that was either directly linked to the person or a metaphor that represented an emotional challenge, for example, that the person experienced.

Similarly, an elephant can recall the scent of a person that they knew or interacted with decades earlier. The extrasensory methods used to *see* that which is *unseeable* to the average human make elephants and humans, or at least Serenity and Alice, begin to have more similarities than differences as was suggested earlier.

We also start to see more examples of people choosing to disappear or avoiding the reality and responsibilities of their lives. Adults appear to be acting like children and Jenna, the child, seems to be acting like an adult. The interaction here between logic, intuition, and maturity points to the growth potential that Serenity, Jenna, and Virgil each have and the potential influence one can have on the other.

Finally, Thomas' character begins to develop a bit besides the broken-down version we were introduced to. He was a leader, hero and advocate for elephants before he ever met Alice and opened a sanctuary to care for them. His mental state points to the immense psychological and emotional suffering he endured at the sanctuary.

Study Questions
How does Serenity, Jenna, and Virgil's behavior and personalities begin to add dimension to the investigative process?

Do their skills hurt or help the investigation?

Describe the similarities between an elephant's and a human's perception and sensitivities. How do these similarities affect Serenity's and Jenna's reality?

Important Terms
Metaphors

Quotations
"…because when you desperately want to believe something's true, you can convince yourself of just about anything"

"You can't blame someone if they honestly don't understand that their reality isn't the same as yours."

Chapter 6-Alice

Alice describes details about elephant experiments that document grief and the recognition of either a dead matriarch from their own herd or a matriarch from an unrelated herd. The studies suggest that elephants are able to recognize and somehow grieve all matriarchs. Some may argue that the studies suggest they are unable to recognize an individual. Alice proposes that maybe all mothers are important.

Analysis

Alice's studies, while professional in nature, continue to suggest that she is self-reflecting. On the one hand, it appears that she is simply stating the facts of an experiment. But she ends the chapter suggesting an alternative conclusion to the usual arguments posed for these particular experiments. These are experiments about elephants. There could be a logical explanation as to why the herd does not distinguish between one elephant matriarch and another. They're elephants who respect their leaders and elders. Had the experiments distinguished between a matriarch and a regular elephant perhaps that would have led to a different conclusion. However, that is not what Alice states. Her statement at the end generalizes all mothers, not simply all elephant mothers. Her statement that perhaps all mothers are important seems like a revelation to her personally rather than simply professionally.

Study Questions

Does it seem as if Alice is developing a greater self-awareness through learning about elephants? How so?

Does her respect for elephants supersede that of humans?

Important Terms

Grief

Quotations

"Some might say if the elephants did not distinguish between the skulls, the fact that one of those skulls was their own mother wasn't important. But maybe it means that all mothers are."

Chapter 7-Virgil

Virgil, the investigator who was on Alice Metcalf's case years earlier, begins this chapter with a story about how all cops have a case that haunts them. One where they make such huge errors of judgment that they believe that they have utterly failed the people involved. Virgil's investigation begins as business-as-usual. But as he probes, he begins to question his boss, Donny, and the decisions he makes during the investigation. Virgil is stunned to learn the real reason Donny refuses to act.

We also learn what happens in the Alice Metcalf disappearance and Nevvie's death-by-elephant trampling. Evidence begins to suggest that the two women may be have been involved in some type of confrontation, but it is unclear why. Nevertheless, we are unable to find out because of Donny's refusal to dig deeper into the case. All we know is that Virgil, formerly known as Victor, knows that Alice checks herself out of the hospital before he has a chance to question her.
Jenna's persistence leads her to find Virgil and the two begin a professional relationship that may or may not lead to the truth of what happened that day.

Analysis
First, notice that a man finally speaks for himself since the story began. In all of the previous chapters, female characters have narrated this story. If a man spoke, it was through the perception of that female narrator. Here, Virgil tells his own story about a case that he believes he has failed. Guilt plagues Virgil's recounting of the Alice Metcalf case. The politics, events, and decisions surrounding that case have so thoroughly disturbed him that he becomes an alcoholic for the remainder of his investigative career so that he can cope with the mistakes he made. He changes his identity and goes from Victor to Virgil, taking on his father's name so that a more positive reputation is bestowed onto him.

Virgil, like Thomas Metcalf, is another male character whose original intentions get clouded and disrupted by events that appear to be beyond their control. They begin as strong-willed, well-intentioned men who later become dysfunctional and utterly unable to care for their well-being.

Virgil mentions the ghost of Alice Metcalf, but not necessarily in the way Serenity has previously defined ghosts, although that type of interpretation may fit here as well. Virgil's ghost, as he tells it, comes from his guilt and his mind. Serenity's definition, as might be analyzed in this chapter, would suggest that Alice may have, in fact, died and her ghost remains in Virgil's life because she still has unfinished business to resolve.

Important Terms
Hallucination

Study Questions
How does Virgil's silence about the sanctuary case destroy him?

How do ghost and spirits play a role in Virgil's life since the Metcalf case?

Quotations

"Every cop has one that got away."

"Be careful what you wish for, sweetheart."

Chapter 8-Alice

Alice's stories begin to delve into memory studies and how memories get stored and filed for future reference. She describes it as an elaborate filing system that allows for complex cross-referencing and codes. She uses elephants as her primary source of data and states that long-term memories are as much for survival purposes as they are for laying the foundation for abstract thought. She ends the chapter with describing an elephant's ability to recall an individual and specific commands that the particular individual taught her.

Analysis

The more often a memory is repeated, the more memory connections that a person or elephant can develop. This means that the stronger the connection that the older file, or set of memories, has to newly developed memories, the more long-lasting those associations become over time.

We now know that Alice was alive that day during the events at the elephant sanctuary and that she checked herself out of the hospital. Her story, up until now, seems to be about elephants and her studies. But this chapter creates a slight turning point. Alice may be alive, but her memory may be the one that is *missing*.

Important Terms

Hippocampus
Serendipitously
Anecdotally

Study Questions

What does Alice's ability to convey complex scientific data in a simple, straight-forward manner say about her?

How do the memory studies relate to her own memories about her past, however vague those stories may be at this point?

Quotations

"You hear, anecdotally, that an elephant never forgets, and I do believe this is true."

"But somewhere, somehow, she remembered who she used to be, too."

Chapter 9-Jenna

Jenna recounts another memory she has of her mother. Here, she recalls the details of a conversation Alice has with a man Jenna assumes is her father. The discussion itself revolves around monogamy within the animal kingdom and whether it exists. Alice believes that the animal kingdom is unable to remain monogamous and believes that it is biologically relevant to engage with many partners.

Jenna's recollection is interrupted by her interaction with Virgil, whom she admits she does not trust. Virgil and Jenna evaluate each other's stories and the claims each makes regarding competency as detectives. After much discussion, Jenna begins to realize that Virgil has a distinct take on the events at the sanctuary, one that Jenna could not and had not developed. Virgil insists that the case was ruled an accident, but that a single red hair was found on Nevvie's body. Both agree that a DNA sample of the hair would be a good first step.

After this meeting, Jenna confronts her grandmother about the events. She wants answers and her forthright nature disturbs the peace. Her grandmother reveals surprising insight and goes into the complicated nature of their mother-daughter relationship.

Analysis
Jenna's quest for the truth about her mother leads her to confront Virgil and her grandmother in a way that disrupts their lives. She wants answers and will persist until she gets them. Although impressive that such a feisty teenager can get to the truth, she shares detailed memories about her mother that point to her genius recollection as a toddler. Further, her life circumstances have caused her to mature far beyond her age. Impressive though she may be, Jenna now doubts the truth of her memory. On the one hand, she wants to face the truth. On the other, there are circumstances that may make her unable or unwilling to accept an un-idealized portrait she has painted of her mom.

Important Terms

Biologically relevant
Anthropomorphize
Extrapolate

Musth
Murder
Chain of Evidence

Study Questions
How does Alice's change of scientific study affect her career?

What kinds of personal circumstances do you believe occurred in her life that would influence her life's work?

Throughout the story, it seems that Alice is narrating for the reader. In this chapter, she uses scientific words without defining them. Could her narration be for someone other than the reader?

Quotations
"Prove to me that monogamy exists in the natural world, without an environmental influence."

"Negative moments get remembered. Traumatic ones get forgotten."

"That's what it's like to be a kid," I say. "No one takes you seriously."

"I wonder if, as you get older, you stop missing people so fiercely. Maybe growing up is just focusing on what you've got, instead of what you don't."

Chapter 10: Alice

Alice begins this chapter with wisdom from Botswana, her place of residence while she conducts fieldwork. She delves into her stories about empathy between elephant mothers and their capacity to empathize with other mothers and their offspring, even if they were another species. Even more unbelievable, she tells a story about an elephant adoption, which, biologically speaking, goes against nature's tendencies because it tends to compromise nurturing their own biological offspring.

Analysis
Alice's narration continues, but in a less scientific manner. Botswana's influence on Alice begins to show as she begins the chapter with a saying that villagers say, but which Alice attributes to the lives of elephants. She continues with anecdotes, not scientific data, which demonstrate that elephants are capable of empathy. Here she is breaking from her role as a scientist and simply speaking as a lay observer of elephants who relies on story-telling to relay data.

She is also breaking away from the other scientists who have begun a large-scale study on scientifically proving elephant empathy. The turning point here indicates that Alice is emotionally changing. She begins to attribute more human-like characteristics to elephants, an uncharacteristic act for a scientist.

Important Terms
Anecdotal evidence
Evolutionary advantage
Empathy
Allomothered

Study Questions
Why do you think that elephants sympathize with other mothers even if it's not biologically feasible?

Discuss Allomothering and how it keeps generations of elephants safe.

What could be the significance of adoption within the elephant community? Could there be a parallel with humans?

Quotations

"Grandmothers in Botswana tell their children that if you want to go quickly, go alone. If you want to go far, you must go together."

"An elephant seems to understand that if you lose a baby, you suffer."

Chapter 11: Serenity

Serenity indulges us with more details about her fame and fortune as a professional psychic. Her relationship with her mother becomes a focal point and her death a turning point in Serenity's psychic career. Serenity's empathy for her clientele, current and future, becomes greater as she begins to personally understand how desperate a person can become to hear from a loved one who has passed. After years of praying, begging, to see her mother, she finally sees her spirit as the youthful woman she was in Serenity's childhood.

This chapter introduces Serenity, Virgil and Jenna to one another. Jenna brings them together in a professional capacity. One has little faith in the other. In spite of what seems to be irreconcilable methods of data collection and beliefs, this group of unorthodox fact-finders manage to find more concrete evidence belonging to Alice. Each also begins to come to terms with certain emotional blind-spots that they had been avoiding up until now.

Analysis
Picoult's method of capitalizing certain words of importance comes into play here. Serenity refers to her psychic ability as a Gift, pointing to the significance it has in her life and, perhaps, existence itself. Nevertheless, Serenity seems to be going out of her way to legitimize her Gift or the existence of the metaphysical world. She speaks of Thomas Edison, world famous inventor, who attempted to create a machine to talk to the dead. These are facts little known to the traditional stories told about Edison such as his invention of the light bulb. Whether her tales convince nonbelievers is unclear, but we do know that Serenity is at the verge of not believing that her Gift will ever return. She might recount such facts to convince herself.
Virgil introduces different theories as to what occurred on that night. He believes that Thomas may have been abusing Alice, suggesting that even if Alice was involved in Nevvie's death, she may have been a victim. His antagonistic style offends Serenity, but the truth is, that Virgil's suspicions are taken seriously.

Important Terms
Reincarnation
Skeptic
Paranormal experiences

Narcissism
Psych Ward
Clairvoyance
Metaphysical
Tsunami of negativity
Fourth Dimension

Study Questions
How do Serenity's spiritual or religious beliefs about reincarnation affect her ability as a psychic? What about her beliefs for human existence? What is Serenity's definition of the meaning of life?

Why would Serenity say that "spirit is genderless"? What distinction is she trying to make between earthly existence as a human and the spirit existence?

What is the fourth dimension?

Quotations
"Spirit is genderless."

"There's a conflict between body and soul, sometimes. That friction is free will."

"The people we define as crazy just might be more sane than you and me."

Chapter 12: Alice

Alice speaks for the first time about her decision to change her doctoral focus to studying elephant grief. She believes she is ridiculed and punished for making that decision, but continues anyway. The punishment comes in the form of entertaining guests, tourists and sightseers. Alice's makes her contempt for that particular job clear. But that assignment is what introduces her to Thomas Metcalf, her future husband. Although reticent at first, she quickly becomes enamored with him.

Analysis
Alice's tale about the day she falls in love with Thomas is told in the present tense. But we now know that Thomas' current reality vastly differs from the tales Alice tells. This, therefore, must be a past account of Alice's life, one which clarifies Alice's stories up to this point in the novel.
Importantly, Thomas is one of few people who agree with Alice's cognitive studies. He gives her advice on how to scientifically justify her cognitive studies with various experiments. He supported her hypotheses on an elephant's ability to grieve. He gives her a fresh perspective on her life, her work, and the grief she has yet to share or make known. While there may be no biological advantage to grief for elephants, there may be one for Alice. Her grief becomes a point of vulnerability with Thomas, who seems to understand her better than anyone she has met. That understanding becomes the starting point for their relationship and romantic life.

Important Terms
Cognition
De facto matriarch
Collaring

Study Questions
How does Alice come to terms with her grief?

Could the de facto matriarch after the death of a female elephant parallel what we have learned about Alice's mother's role after her disappearance?

Quotations

"You're going to have to let her go," I said out loud, but I am not sure which one of us I was trying to convince."

"There is a difference between the romance of Africa and the reality of it."

"There's no biological advantage to grief."

Chapter 13: Jenna

Jenna, Serenity, and Virgil take a trip to visit Thomas Metcalf in the institution. They arrive at a purple palace and find him fighting with the orderlies because he believes they are going to take his research, which is really just a cereal box. Jenna enters the room and Thomas mistakes her for Alice, his wife. Jenna manages to calm him down, but her friends have witnessed everything and they are disturbed. Thomas continues to speak to *Alice* about his research until Virgil forces him to acknowledge that it's Jenna. For a brief moment, Thomas does until he sees the necklace that Jenna is wearing. That is the necklace that Jenna found belonging to Alice. Thomas' thunderous slap across *Alice's face* scares everybody. The orderlies come in to sedate him.

Analysis

The trio visit Metcalf in the psychiatric institution to gather more details about the murder and disappearance. They quickly realize that Thomas still believes that his present is a decade earlier when his wife was still in his life. He begins by talking about a theory he has been developing about elephant's theory of mind. This theory makes logical sense and reminds Jenna of his intelligence. Nevertheless, he strangely confuses Jenna for Alice until Virgil forces him to see her, both as an individual and to visually recognize her as Jenna. Jenna's likeness of Alice haunts Thomas. It is as if she, Alice, is Thomas' ghost whom Jenna embodies. The trio receives a substantial amount of information that lead each to gather more data to support their theories. Thomas's extreme emotions from happily hugging *Alice,* to tenderly hugging Jenna, then to violently slapping *Alice* clearly demonstrate his instability.

Important Terms
Purple inspires healing
Theory of mind
Mirror neurons

Study Questions
Discuss how Virgil and Serenity use the information they have discovered to build their theories about this case.

How does this particular instance of instability bring the reality of the situation into focus for Jenna?

Has Thomas' mental illness affected his intelligence?

Quotations:
"Alice, you cannot imagine what I've just discovered!"

Chapter 14: Alice

Alice begins by describing a ritual or act that elephants engage in-the dusting and covering up of a dead animal or one that can be perceived as dead. She has difficulty determining whether this is a ritual to respect the dead or an act that can mean something else. At one point, she falls asleep under a tree where the elephant bones are buried. She is startled when she finds that elephants have covered her in leaves, too. After, Alice announces that she is ten weeks pregnant.

Analysis
Alice seems to believe that the act of dusting and covering an elephant up with leaves is a ritual that elephants engage in when they are acknowledging the death of someone. But Alice's comment about being *more than herself* suggest a spiritual experience-perhaps one where the mind or brainpower is overtaken by something else like hormones.

Important Terms
Musth/Madness
Mahout

Study Questions
Besides a death or grieving ritual, could the elephant's behavior be about something else?

How can Alice be so sure she is witnessing a death ritual?

Why would the ritual be reserved only for aggressive or unexpected deaths?

Quotations
"I have a story that is not one of my own . . ."

"I was more than myself. I've always found it ironic that the elephants which found me sleeping assumed I was dead, when in reality I was full of life."

Chapter 15: Serenity

We return to the scene at the institution, but from Serenity's point of view. She cannot believe the sheer strength of Thomas' hand which causes Jenna to fly across the room. Virgil slaps him back.

Analysis
This is a threshold chapter which signifies a turning point for each of the characters. Serenity accepts that what Jenna may need more than anything is a mother-like figure to guide her through this investigation. She also begins to understand that she has some investigative tips to give Virgil. Rather than state a conclusion and fit the facts to the theory, she suggests that Virgil allow the facts to speak for themselves. Serenity becomes the voice of reason.

Jenna begins to realize that her theories may have been all wrong. She learns more about her father's violent strength, scientific intelligence, and what may have been his role in the murder/disappearance. She learns that her mother may have been abused and that she may have had an affair-truths she has never considered.

Important Terms

Hysterical strength
Somatic intuition

Quotations

"I am not a mother, but maybe that's what I'm supposed to be right now for this girl."

"As soon as I cross the threshold, it's easier to breathe."

Chapter 16: Alice

Alice shares more stories about a mother elephant's extraordinary love and patience for its babies. She begins to share more details about how baby elephants are raised by the herd and how they are protected all the while alluding to her own experience and self-reflection.

Analysis

Alice begins to define certain terms used for her elephant research. She has not yet, up to this point, been defining the words. One may suspect that if she wanted or needed the reader to understand her stories, she would have defined them from the beginning. That is, unless she was only writing for herself, in which case she would have no need to define them.

Important Terms
Allomothering

Study Questions
Why does Alice begin to define key words in her research and studies at this point?

She has no real need to define them. For whom do you believe she now speaks to?

Why does she believe that elephant mothers are patient beyond belief?

Quotations
"In the wild, a mother and daughter stay together until one of them dies."

Chapter 17: Jenna

Jenna is walking home after the fiasco that occurred at the institution. She's angry, hurt, and probably confused about what she has learned. Serenity begs her into the car so that she can take her home. She begins to realize that there are volumes more to her mother's disappearance than she was first able to grasp.

Jenna's realization that both of her parent's may have been involved the evening of the sanctuary shocks her to her core. She had always believed that her parents were happily married. The fact that they may not have been crushes her naïve assumptions about her life, her mom's life and the reality of who her family was. She comes to terms with the idea that Gideon may have been either her biological father or her adoptive father, which exactly remains to be seen.

Analysis
Jenna's return to the former sanctuary and the purple mushrooms signify her desire or inspiration to move towards healing. The purple mushrooms were created after the burial of an elephant at the sanctuary suggesting that elephants can play and have played a healing role in her life and the lives of her family members.

Important Terms
Purple mushrooms

Study Questions
How do facts factor into this chapter? Is a fact simply a fact? Or, is it subject to interpretation and re-interpretation?

Does the team effort clarify or confuse the investigation?

Quotations
"Can a person hold tightly to two thoughts that look, at first sight, as if they'd cancel each other out?"

". . . I love that she doesn't apologize for herself . . ."

"[A]ll the universe wants from us is two things: Don't do any intentional harm to yourself or anyone else, and get happy."

Part II
Chapter 18: Alice

In this chapter, Alice describes the difficulty in determining whether an elephant is pregnant. At the same time, she longs to understand her relationship with Thomas and whether it would be a long-lasting one rather than just a one night stand. Alice discovers that she is pregnant and decides that it is time to pay Thomas a visit in New Hampshire at the New England Elephant Sanctuary. She takes time off from her research in Botswana and reconnects with Thomas in New Hampshire.

After sharing details about daily life at the Elephant Sanctuary versus the African game reserve, we see that Alice is introduced to the Sanctuary family, both human and elephant. She longs to plant roots and have a home and family for herself and the baby. Alice's first impression convinces her that her future is at the Sanctuary, at once familiar and strange.

Analysis
Alice remarks about a mother elephant's excellent parenting skills. But when she speaks of herself, she seems to believe that she has a choice about motherhood, a choice to have a child or not. The scene is set in New Hampshire where Alice meets new elephants, including Asian elephants, and a new member of the family, Maura. The new beginnings that Alice encounters both challenges her with a new context and a new scenario to study elephant grief. It also provides with a new elephant and human family. This seems to be the idyllic beginning of her friendships and her relationship with Thomas.

Important Terms
Micromanaging
Behavior Modification

Study Questions
Discuss Alice's seemingly rhetorical question about whether a woman can still call herself a mother after losing a child.

Compare elephant and human mothers. What makes an elephant's parenting skills distinct from a human mother's? What makes them similar?

How does Maura the elephant's arrival overlap with Alice's arrival and decision to stay?

Quotations
"If you are a mother, you must have someone to take care of. If that someone is taken from you, whether it is a newborn or an individual old enough to have offspring of its own, can you still call yourself a mother?"

"… I realized that she hadn't just lost her calf. She had lost herself."

"[E]lephant mothers put human ones to shame."

Chapter 19: Virgil

Virgil recounts his role in the Alice Metcalf disappearance and the
Nevvie Ruehl death. He reviews the evidence left in his office with a
renewed vigor. He sees things within the evidence that he had previously
overlooked, including DNA evidence. His energy for reviewing this case
is refreshed by the idea that he may be able to rectify a series of errors
that he made when he was on the case a decade earlier.
He decides to team up with Serenity. Together, they negotiate their
boundaries and respect for one another's talents. They decide to
investigate former establishments to see if anyone may have information
related to the incidents. They learn quite a bit about Gideon and Grace,
more than they expected so many years later. Both are re-energized in a
way they have not been in in years and they agree that they must fix what
they had done wrong.

Analysis
Here, we learn that Virgil has deep regrets about the way he handled the
death and disappearance at the Sanctuary ten years ago. In order to
regain his confidence and guide his *way*, we see that he concedes by
teaming up with a psychic, Serenity. Although he is certain that she does
not engage in a credible method of investigation, he appears to be
compelled to contact her not only to help Jenna, but each other and
themselves.

Important Terms
Detritus
Threshold
Paranormal
Clairvoyant
Charlatan

Study Questions
Why does Virgil feel so compelled to right this wrong of his past?

Name some similarities and differences between a psychic and detective.
Are they both really different?

How do Virgil's faults diminish or add to his credibility?

Quotations

"Rage often brings out the real person."

"Detectives are observers."

Chapter 20: Alice

Alice continues to discuss elephant motherhood and the huge investment in time and resources that an elephant makes to have a baby. She describes her spiritual connection and affinity towards Maura, the new elephant at the sanctuary who they learn is pregnant. In Botswana, Alice had witnessed the birth of a baby elephant, an experience she describes as incredible. This was Alice's first birth at the Sanctuary. Everyone was excited, but to their dismay, the baby elephant is stillborn.

We are introduced to conflicts between Nevvie and Alice and to strange behavior by Thomas which scares Alice. After the baby elephant dies, Nevvie and Alice's conflict escalates as both experts attempt to assert their authority over the immediate burial of the elephant versus allowing Maura to grieve until she chooses to stop.

Analysis
Much like the Asian and African elephants that must be separated in captivity, Alice and Nevvie must also be separated within the sanctuary. Primarily, each of their experiences and expertise with elephants dictates their beliefs about how to deal with the stillborn elephant. The conflict is both started and resolved by Thomas who undergoes psychological changes which scare Alice, but seem to be controllable with pills.

Choice begins to factor heavily in each of the character's lives, including Maura. Making their own choices is held in high regard for Alice, whereas Nevvie is perfectly ok with imposing her decisions. This becomes a critical point in their professional and personal relationships.

Important Terms
Anthropomorphic

Study Questions
Why does Alice grieve the stillborn birth as if her own child had died?

Describe Thomas' appearance and behavior and how it is similar to Alice's.

How does Nevvie impose human emotion onto Maura?

Quotations
"You separated a grieving mother from her calf?"

Chapter 21: Jenna

Jenna boldly escapes New Hampshire by greyhound to Tennessee. By this point, she realizes that Gideon may still be at the Tennessee sanctuary. She reviews her theories as to what Gideon's role may be in the murder/disappearance and proceeds to do what she can to learn more. She turns off her cell phone to avoid contact with everyone including her Grandmother, whom she is certain will not be happy.

Analysis
Jenna's uses the belief of her invisibility as an advantage. She believes that people do not notice kids. This gives her a sense of freedom to observe anything she wants and to go where she chooses. The theme of choice is reinforced here as it is in other chapters with Alice and Nevvie. Jenna seems to have given herself permission to choose how to resolve this crucial matter. Her resolve to get closure and to know what happened to her mother seems to be limitless.

Important Terms
Catatonic

Study Questions

Discuss Jenna's persistence to find her mother.

What kind of audacity does it take for Jenna to go to Tennessee by herself?

Are there similarities between Alice and Jenna's temperaments?

How does the theme of choice affect Alice, Jenna, and the elephants?

Quotations
"When you're a kid, most people actively go out of their way to not notice you."

"See, that's the other thing about people who think kids are invisible: They forget to be careful around you."

"Pay Attention."

Chapter 22: Alice

Alice describes the elaborate mating rituals that elephants engage in. She begins with gestures and continues with the vocalizations that complement the behavior. Elephants, especially the female, have a limited amount of time to attract potential mates, so the female must sing with a roar to ensure she attracts a male. She ends by wondering whether these calls are passed down from generation-to-generation, from mother to daughter.

Analysis
Although Alice tries not to impose human emotion or behavior on elephant behavior, it seems as if she is compelled to try, at least theoretically, to impose elephant behavior onto humans. She continues to speak as if by studying elephants, she will learn something about herself and her future. It is unclear, however, what she will learn.

Important Terms
Musth male
Female in estrus
Estrus Song
Pheromones

Study Questions
What is the significance of describing elephant mating rituals?

Why do you think Alice uses whales as a comparison to elephants?

What can the reader anticipate about mother-daughter relationships, either elephant or human?

Alice refers to generational mother-daughter relationships. By doing so, does she allude to her relationship with her own mother?

Quotations
"...for elephants, mating is a song and dance."

"If, by doing this, the daughters learn from their mothers' mistakes."

Chapter 23: Serenity

Serenity confesses to the reader that she is no longer able to communicate with spirits, but finds it hard to admit that to Virgil and Jenna. Virgil and Serenity come up with plausible alternatives to understand what may have happened to Alice, Nevvie, Gideon, and Grace. They suspect that Alice and Gideon were having an affair, but decide that they must go to the Sanctuary in Tennessee to find out more. Before leaving, they decide to contact or visit Jenna, but both attempts fail. It dawns on Virgil that Jenna may already be on her way.

Analysis
Virgil and Serenity appear to be a more cohesive team. They seem to be developing a bond that allows for more respectable dialogue and exchange of ideas. They challenge each other's ideas and take the investigation more seriously as the stakes appear to become higher than before. This becomes especially true when they realize that Jenna may have left to Tennessee without them.

Important Terms
Suicides
Ghosts

Study Questions
Why does Serenity begin with a tale about the ghost of a man who committed suicide?

Whom does she believe may have committed suicide?

How is this significant to what happened at the Sanctuary?

Quotations
"Talking to spirits is a dialogue. It takes two. If you're trying hard and coming up empty, it's either because of a spirit who won't communicate or because of a medium who can't."

"Suicides, almost by definition, are all ghosts"

Chapter 24: Alice

Alice describes elephant grief as a fact of their lives, but one that is not feasible to their survival, especially in the wild. A grieving elephant may not be capable of caring for its safety or survival as a species. Grieving must occur quickly and the animal must continue with its life for the sake of its survival.

Alice goes on to describe Thomas' change in behavior that looks like the opposite of his previous catatonic and angry state. His fast talking and unusual need for sex are odd, but not alarming. Not until Thomas breaks the bank does Alice become alarmed about the second mortgage on the house and his heavy spending on an ill-timed business idea. She finally discovers and admits that Thomas is very sick and requires professional attention.

Finally, Grace admits to Alice that she is unable to have children, but she is unable to tell Gideon the truth. In the meantime, she loves caring for baby Jenna without taking responsibility for telling Gideon the truth.

Analysis
Many truths come out in this chapter. Alice is forced to recognize these truths whether she wants to or not. The most painful of all is the fact that she has made serious error in judgment by marrying Thomas because she does not confront the signs of his mental illness sooner. Thomas' violence scares Alice into action. Most profoundly, she finds comfort in her friendship with Maura the elephant.

Important Terms

Evolutionarily feasible
Viscous sadness
Catatonic
Feral
Tethered
Molecular Consolidation Theory
Fourth dimension
Baptism

Study Questions
What has Thomas already mentioned about Alice's studies on elephant cognition and memory and her use of his research?

What could the codes represent for Thomas? Could he be claiming ownership of those chemical formulas by writing them down?

Quotations
"If memories protected us from future dangerous situations, was it in our best interests to chemically forget them?"

"Where there is support, there is no grief."

Chapter 25: Virgil

Virgil and Serenity make their way to Tennessee. After overcoming some challenges, they reach Tennessee and find G. Cartwright in the phone book. They visit the address and find the home of Grace Cartwright. They encounter Nevvie and confusion sets in about her death and Alice's disappearance. As they speak with Nevvie, she mentions Grace and it seems that Grace may not have died or committed suicide either.

Analysis
This chapter throws confusion at the reader as to the legitimate facts of the case. Nevvie makes statements that confuse Serenity and Virgil. The strange occurrence of the weeping house further confuses and terrifies them. They are no longer confident that they know what has happened and believe that Thomas may have lied about everything that night. By questioning their assumptions about the facts, Serenity and Virgil are forced to view the case from a fresh perspective.
Trust takes on a different meaning when Virgil questions whether Thomas had too much control in shaping the story that night. He believed Thomas at face value and begins to realize that he trusted Thomas' story too easily. Doubt creeps into his mind.

Important Terms
Weeping house

Study Questions
What significance does a weeping house have in this chapter?

How is truth revealed here as compared to other chapters? Must it be investigated? Or, could the truth lie directly in the characters' faces, which they are refusing to acknowledge?

Quotations
"Just remember, no matter what happens, you'll get there eventually."

"— tracks that are rapidly vanishing in the heat, as if we were never there at all."

Chapter 26: Alice

Thomas has been away for two months. Alice takes over business operations at the Elephant Sanctuary and the Sanctuary staff is adjusting to the new reality. Gideon begins to take on more responsibility and Maura has found a way to move on from her baby's death. As she moves past it, Maura and Hester develop a friendship at the same time that Alice and Gideon develop an intimate one. To their surprise, Thomas returns to the sanctuary prepared to make amends.

Analysis

With Thomas gone, it seems as if the staff and elephants begin to have more light-hearted fun. Maura and Hester become playful giants and the intimacy between Gideon and Alice grows stronger. Even Grace, always a little out-of-place, has discovered a pleasure in caring for Jenna. Thomas' absence causes the Sanctuary to have a little fun even as their financial concerns threaten the Sanctuary's existence. It appears that a hopeful future is possible until Thomas shows up at their cottage.

Important Terms

Compartmentalize

Trust

Scientific Credibility

Study Questions

The sanctuary staff appears to adjust to Thomas' absence and seems to be moving on with their lives. Is this based on their reality or is this a form of denial?

What kind of trust issues come up in this chapter between: Alice and Thomas; Gideon and Grace; the Sanctuary with local businesses?

What kind of currency does trust have?

Quotations

"In two months, you can start over."

"What I think is that there is no perspective in grief, or in love."

Chapter 27: Jenna

Jenna finds her way to the Elephant Sanctuary in Tennessee. By a great stroke of luck, Gideon is one of the first people she see and speaks to. She immediately begins asking him questions about her mother and where she could be. She learns that her mother had planned to take Jenna and run. But Gideon never heard from Alice again, so he did not know as much as Jenna had hoped. He did, however, offer new information that shocked Jenna. Gideon mentions that Alice had been pregnant at the time of her disappearance, presumably with his child. Stunned by that bit of news, Jenna begins to suspect that Gideon may have killed her mother to hide the pregnancy from his wife. Such suggestions, though, upset Gideon and Jenna realizes that she may have gone too far. She immediately contacts Serenity for help.

Analysis
Jenna's desperate need for information about the case leads her to Gideon. She questions the ease with which she reaches the Elephant Sanctuary and with finding Gideon. She comes to believe that she is finally getting the break she needs to uncover the truth.

Important Terms
Positive and negative reinforcement

Free Contact

Electroluminescent

Apparated

Study Questions
Is Jenna getting the cosmic break she's been praying for?

How does positive reinforcement help elephants who have developed serious trust issues with humans?

How did negative reinforcement make them that way?

How does positive reinforcement factor in the lives of Serenity, Alice, and Jenna in the story?

What does apparated mean?

Quotations

"All of a sudden, my body is infused with light."

Chapter 28: Alice

Thomas has been at the Sanctuary for 5 months and has transitioned into his professional role well. But his relationship with Alice continues to suffer and deteriorate, particularly as all parties involved become aware of her affair with Gideon. After much turmoil and regret, Alice begins to plan her escape. She dreams of running away from Thomas and the Sanctuary, but on the day she decides to take action the group learns of Grace's death.

Analysis
This chapter becomes a turning point in the lives of everyone at the Sanctuary. Trust that already been broken becomes known to all parties involved. Thomas' increasing aggression towards Alice frightens her and her decision to leave is not taken lightly. The power struggles cause a serious imbalance within the Sanctuary as the truth hurts everyone.

Important Terms
Manic or depressive episode
Vicious cycle
Monsoon/cleansing/storm
Liar

Study Questions
What do the different images of water represent in this story?

Does the truth hurt people or is it the denial of the truth that causes pain?

Quotations
"What judge would think of you as a fit mother?" he hissed."

"This was their home, maybe more than it ever had been mine. I began to plan my escape."

Chapter 29: Serenity

Serenity and Virgil are still reeling from their encounter with the weeping house. Seeing Nevvie shocked them, but witnessing what Serenity now calls a water poltergeist terrifies them. They run until they find Jenna who shares what she has learned from Gideon. The three put all the new pieces of information together and begin to dissect the fact that Nevvie was still alive.

Analysis
The first acknowledgement that Jenna and Virgil are not from this world is made. We begin to wonder what has occurred in the previous chapters compared to what has occurred in this one. Virgil has driven off of a cliff that he seems to have survived and Jenna is *at the end*, but it is unclear why. The reader may not have specific details, but the truth continues to come out about Virgil and Jenna's existence. Serenity also admits she is a *hack*, a fraudulent psychic. But instead of running, Virgil and Serenity are more determined than ever to make things right for Jenna.

Important Terms
Water poltergeist

Study Questions
Who could Serenity be speaking to?

How does Grace's ghost fight back? Is that all she accomplishes?

Quotations
"The spirit world is modeled on the real world, and the real things we've seen."

"It's no small feat, finishing a journey," I tell her."

"Serenity," Jenna asks. "Will you let me talk to her whenever I need to?"

"He's flawed, and scarred, and battle-weary, just like me. Just like all of us."

Chapter 30: Alice

We find the Sanctuary team mourning Grace's loss, but attempting to find normalcy by continuing to care for the elephants. During that time, Alice helps Gideon on a short two-person fence-mending job and decides to leave Jenna alone while she slept. When she returns to the cottage, she is unable to find Jenna and panics. Gideon finally finds her in Nevvie's arms. Alice is comforted, but continues to discuss the strange behavior of an elephant who tried to kidnap a baby elephant from its mother. Additionally, she has a nightmare about Grace's suicide. Alice connects none of this, however, to her psychic intuition or to her pregnancy.

Analysis
The truth continues to disrupt the characters' lives. We learn that Gideon is not sorry that Grace is gone. This might point to the fact that he, too, was tired of living a lie and that he was unable to discuss that with Grace. Alice, Grace, and Gideon seem to have believed that by hiding their secrets they were preventing the risk of losing their spouses. But the exact opposite has occurred and this chapter shows that their secrets have had grave consequences.

Important Terms
Protective home
Leaving Time

Study Questions
What does Leaving Time mean? Why might a child like Jenna call sleeping Leaving Time?

Why are the words 'secrets' and 'bliss' used in the same sentence?

Do the secrets protect anyone except the ones abusing their discretion?

How do Alice's nightmares relate to her pregnancy and Jenna's idea of Leaving Time?

Quotations
"We'd had a year of secrets, a year of bliss. What had happened to Grace was the punishment, the payment due."

"Jenna called it the Leaving Time."

"I was thinking about how my nights had been dark and dreamless my whole life, except for one notable exception, when my imagination kicked into overdrive and every midnight hour was a pantomime of my greatest fears."

Chapter 31: Jenna

Jenna finally returns to her grandmother who is extremely upset and relieved to see Jenna again. Grandma sends Jenna to her room and she continues to process all of the information she has gathered. She begins to understand that her father may have killed her mom, but is relieved that she did not purposely leave her behind. Later, Jenna and her grandmother argue about taking her investigation too far. Her grandmother yanks all of the research from Jenna's hands and demands that she begin to live her own life. Jenna throws a tantrum, but later deletes the Missing Persons report that she filed online.

Analysis
Jenna's understanding of reality begins to cause confusion for the reader. She has previously admitted to Serenity that she is on *the other side*. But Jenna speaks as if she is a middle school teenager who continues to live her life as a living human being. It seems that Jenna is moving between two worlds, but it is unclear why or how she is able to navigate both.

Important Terms

Kaleidoscope
Implode
Stricken ship
Closure
Institutionalized

Study Questions
Why does it seem as if Jenna is still alive after she has already spoken about being on the other side?

What role is Serenity playing for Jenna? How about her grandmother?

Quotations
"She did not willingly leave me behind."

"Until now, I hadn't realized that words have sharp edges; that they can cut your tongue."

"No prison is going to be more punishing than the confines of his own mind."

"I move like the wind; I feel invisible."

Chapter 32: Alice

Truths continue to burst the bubbles of denial within the family. Gideon tells Nevvie that Alice is pregnant. Alice tells Thomas, too, and admits that she is leaving the Sanctuary with Gideon. Thomas' violence escalates as he smacks Alice and draws blood. He tells Alice to go ahead and leave, but makes it abundantly clear that she will not take Jenna from him.

Analysis
Gideon has had enough of hiding and tells Nevvie that Alice is pregnant. This forces Alice to confront Thomas as well, but with much graver consequences. Alice's fear of Thomas becomes reality as he uses physical violence to demonstrate his anger. Alice is then left to run for her life and for help because she no longer trusts that Thomas will not hurt Jenna. Instead of leaving on her own terms, she leaves under threat of violence and fear.

Important Terms
Dream out loud in Technicolor
Fantasy

Study Questions
What effect does the truth have on Nevvie and Thomas? How do their reactions correspond with what Gideon and Alice had hoped would happen?

Is it accurate or fair to attribute Thomas' violence to his mental illness?

Quotations
"Resolve is like porcelain, isn't it?"

Chapter 33: Virgil

Virgil thinks about how he can obtain information about the body. He realizes that there is an autopsy report he may be able to read. He connects with his main points of contact in the police department and the DNA lab, but does not learn much from them. He, Serenity, and Jenna continue to discuss the evidence and new theories about each person's involvement in the death and disappearance. By the end of this chapter, it is quite possible that Virgil is beginning to understand and accept Serenity's psychic abilities.

Analysis

The most telling and interesting part of this chapter are the strange looks that Serenity receives from outsiders, third parties who are witnessing her behavior in the diner. It is unclear why they give her these looks. Perhaps this team of investigators is much stranger than it appears.

Important Terms
Metaphysical

Sliver of hope

Study Questions
Why do you think the restaurant diners look at Serenity and the team in a strange way?

What makes endings so critical in this story?

Quotations
"[T]here is no greater force on earth than a mother's revenge."

"Endings are critical."

Chapter 34: Alice

Alice describes why infants cannot remember events. She links their inability to use language as the main reason. However, in an emergency situation, an infant can still communicate its fear by shrieking a specific cry that is available only in those times.

Analysis
Alice seems to be having either a premonition or is anticipating something happening to her child or a child. She recounts an infant's ability to communicate in emergency situations as a matter of fact. No one has been hurt yet, but we can sense the impending danger.

Important Terms

Extreme distress
Abject terror
Amygdala/ larynx
Heliotrope

Study Questions

Alice seems to be talking about a human child. Which infant might she be referring to?

Who could place a child in extreme distress?

Quotations
"In fact, the noise you'll make is one you probably could not replicate voluntarily if you tried."

Chapter 35: Serenity

Jenna, Virgil and Serenity return to a spot at the former elephant sanctuary that Alice considered special. Together, they channel energy and Serenity says a prayer so that Jenna can finally communicate with her mother. She guides Jenna to speak to her mother as if she were living. Serenity realizes that it is that simple, but decides that she needs to sound the alarm so that Jenna gets an immediate response. Like a miracle, Serenity is poked by a tooth that has been hiding under the soil where she sits.

Analysis
From one chapter to the next, it seems that Alice is tipping Serenity off with information about the significance of a child's cry. Serenity intuitively understands that this shriek, a cry that can only happen during an emergency situation, is the only thing that will cause Alice to respond. She begins to realize, too, that Jenna has a responsibility to accept reality, whatever that may be. She must be ready to listen. But it is unclear what Jenna will hear.

Important Terms
Open channeling
Ethereal
Purple mushrooms

Study Questions
Is Serenity beginning to realize that finding Alice means that Jenna must be ready to listen? How does she realize this? Ready to listen to what?

Quotations
"I don't know if you can miss someone you can barely remember, but that's how I feel."

"Sometimes the universe gives you a gift."

"What would make a mother pay attention? Her child's cry."

"This is about energy," I say. "That's how spirits manifest."

"[M]aybe her mother has been trying to communicate with her all along, but until now, she was unwilling to accept the fact that Alice was dead. Maybe she's finally ready to listen."

Chapter 36: Alice

Alice continues to discuss emergency situations and how a traumatic death can affect the future of baby elephants in the wild. We learn that a traumatized elephant will behave in strange ways that not only endangers the safety and care of a baby elephant, but can endanger humans as well.

Analysis

Alice's distinction between natural death and murder suggests that the aftereffects can have grave consequences for everyone involved, especially elephants whose excellent memory does not allow them to forget such abuse and trauma.

Important Terms

Parental guidance
Trauma
Culling

Study Questions

What does Alice suggest about memory and trauma in elephants?

How we can compare this information to a human who undergoes trauma?

How significant is parental guidance for the survival of an elephant herd?

Quotations

"But when there is no family to teach a young female to raise her own calf, things can go horribly awry."

"At the very least, it is crucial when studying the grief of elephants to remember that death is a natural occurrence. Murder is not."

Chapter 37: Jenna

Jenna, Virgil, and Serenity quickly go to visit Tallulah about analyzing the tooth. Virgil tells her that he would prefer she analyze the tooth instead of the dried blood on the shirt. Tallulah surprises them by immediately identifying the tooth as a baby human tooth. We do not know whose tooth it could be yet, but Jenna immediately launches into a memory about a pain she experienced-a pain that she vividly recalls. Jenna knows that she is being held by someone other than her mother or father. She begins to cry when the stranger's hand firmly covers Jenna's mouth. Later, we find that Maura has taken Jenna somewhere and begins to cover her with branches.

Analysis
Alice has revealed countless rituals that grieving elephants undergo and the process by which an elephant buries their dead. Jenna's description of what has occurred suggests that her memory is that of being covered by Maura, the elephant, as she would if she were burying a baby elephant.

Important Terms
Pain that erupts in my mouth
Stars exploding where my eyes were
Raw shimmering nerve

Study Questions

What is Jenna experiencing? What does her memory suggest?

Why does she lose contact with Serenity?

If we know that Serenity is alive, why might she lose contact with Jenna?

Quotations

"Sometimes the connection was crystal clear, and sometimes it was like being on a cell phone in the mountains, where you only catch every third word, Serenity had said."

Chapter 38: Alice

Alice discusses two deaths. The first is that of her daughter Jenna. Alice admits to having seen Jenna's dead body, but she chooses not to call police because she feared that they would come after her. The second death is that of her mother, who had died of cancer long before Jenna was born. Alice's mother's death changed the course of her career, academic focus, and life.

Analysis

Alice's impersonal discussion of her daughter seems matter-of-fact and without sufficient emotion for a grieving daughter. She admits that she misses her child and that her life will never be normal again, but she confesses that she chose self-preservation over risking being arrested. The death of her mother, on the other hand, changes the course of her life. Feeling all alone afterwards, Alice longs for a family or support system of her own. She witnesses how supportive elephants are within the herd.

There is an element of guilt more than grief here. Alice observes the way elephants teach each other how to mother a baby elephant. They spend years cultivating their daughters' parenting skills, all of which Alice does not appear to have learned from her own mother.

Important Terms

Poachers
En masse

Study Questions

Does it appear that Alice experiences guilt more than grief over Jenna's death?

Discuss Alice's reaction to seeing her daughter's body.

Compare and contrast the way that Alice describes parenting skills within an elephant herd and what we've read so far about her relationship with her mother.

Quotations

"…the canyon between who I used to be and who I was now would be so broad that I wouldn't be able to see the far side."

"When an elephant calf loses its family, you must provide a new one."

"Nothing will ever be normal again."

"After all, we raise our own children to live without us, one day. It's when they leave us too soon that nothing makes sense."

Chapter 39: Virgil

Virgil confronts his reality by re-analyzing the facts of his existence. He rigorously questions why he swipes through people and why he seems so invisible to some people, but not to others. He recalls the day of his suicide and attempts to piece things together after he drives off the cliff. His connection to Jenna, Tallulah, and all of the others he encounters seems to flicker on an off. But he realizes that his connection to Serenity is strong and constant.

Analysis
Here we encounter another moment of recognizing the truth of his reality. Virgil begins to understand that he may have died. Death here is described by Serenity as being similar to sleeping. She walks Virgil through the process even though she appears to be alive. We are also introduced to the idea that Virgil becomes aware that his mind controls his location.

Important Terms

Suspended animation

Study Questions

Is it possible that Virgil is only now beginning to understand that he has, in fact, died?

Is it possible that all of his encounters with everyone has been with other ghosts or spirits?

Who is alive in this story and who is dead?

How powerful is Virgil's mind if he is able to think and suddenly appear at any given location?

Quotations

"In this world, but not of it."

"But I am suddenly so light and weightless that I don't even have to move, I just think and I'm where I need to be. I blink, and I can see her."

Chapter 40: Alice

Alice proceeds with describing her loss and the death of a third, fourth and possibly fifth person. She verifies that she checked herself out of the hospital on that fateful night and that she knew she had miscarried by that point. Further, she confesses that she looked up Gideon's whereabouts and learns that he died during the Iraq war. Additionally, she believes that Alice Metcalf, the great elephant researcher, symbolically died on the day she ran from the Sanctuary. As she recalls her story, she receives a phone call from New Hampshire. The call is from a cop who tells her that they have found Jenna's remains.

Analysis

Within a span of hours, Alice loses Jenna, her unborn child, Gideon, and her husband. Alice suddenly loses the family she longed for and the support she wished she had. Alice reminisces about her old life from the new reserve in South Africa. Her life in Botswana and New Hampshire now appear to be of another life, another woman. Her new beginning is with a new set of orphaned elephants that she trains to re-integrate into their own society. What she cannot seem to do with humans, she becomes an expert at for elephants. She remains anonymously supportive of the Elephant Sanctuary in Tennessee and hangs on to mementos that remind her of that life. But she chooses to remain distant and invisible to the Sanctuary.

Important Terms

Self-destruction

Study Questions

Who is alive and who is dead at this point in the story?

What do the previous chapters tell us about the cast of characters in this story?

Does the fact that they are spirits, ghosts or poltergeists make them any less alive, real or significant?

What has Jenna suggested in previous chapters about Maura's artwork? She claims to be able to read script that Maura has stripped onto the bark. What has she alluded to regarding Maura's ability to communicate?

Quotations

"The worst part of my day is when it is over."

"When I wake up, I am screaming. I do not like to sleep, and if I must, I want it to be thick and dreamless."

Chapter 41: Serenity

Serenity, too, comes to terms with everything that has occurred with the investigation and her relationships with Virgil, Jenna, and Tallulah. She begins to understand that she is alone, although everyone felt very real to her. As she retraces her steps, she encounters the waitress who waited her table at the diner. Serenity questions what the waitress saw and the waitress hands her the contact information for a mental health center.

Serenity then engages in a complete review of every character she has encountered and begins to realize that almost everyone is dead. Her sense of reality is shaken, but in reviewing her circumstances, she begins to understand that those considered mentally ill and young children can also see what she sees.

Finally, Desmond and Lucinda return to Serenity's life and begin to help her again now that she has regained her self-confidence.

Analysis

We know that Serenity's results to uncover the truth   has legitimate consequences for Alice, whom Serenity finally meets. Serenity's efforts provides closure for everyone. She uncovers authentic evidence and validates and corroborates the evidence that Virgil and Jenna have guided her towards. But the means by which she does so is considered illegitimate and lacking credibility. She begins to understand that there is a very thin divide between the living and the dead, the sane and the insane.

Important Terms

Skeptic

Study Questions

How would you react to a person who claims to be a psychic?

Would you wait to understand whether they are legitimate or would you waive them off as charlatans?

We have already determined that most everyone in the story is dead. Does that mean that Serenity was alone?

Quotations

"I can't tell who is alive and who isn't, so I look down at the ground, refusing to make eye contact."

"My head buzzes. It's like the beginning of a migraine, but I think it is actually the sound of everything I know, everything I believed, being challenged."

Chapter 42: Alice

After some thought, Alice decides to give Jenna's remains a proper burial. She hesitates before doing so, but decides to confront her past. She even has the strength and courage to visit Thomas at the mental institution. She longs for his support, but finds that he is lost and trapped by the past. Her encounter with Serenity is difficult and violent. The clash between logic and Serenity's psychic ability occurs, but Alice succumbs and chooses to hear what Serenity has to say.

Analysis
Alice's confession to Serenity about what happens that night comes spilling out. After her rage subsides at Serenity's perceived mockery of the case, Alice understands that Serenity is one of the few people able to piece together crucial missing pieces of the entire story.

Important Terms

Rage
Nightmare
Pitch black
Anguish

Study Questions
Why does Alice feel compelled to visit Thomas?

How does Alice find closure with Serenity?

Does acceptance of what happened provide sufficient closure?

Quotations

"Instead, I found Thomas so trapped by the past that he can't accept the future."

"Rage rises in me like a geyser."

"Ninety-eight percent of science is quantifiable… That is the 2 percent of science that can't be measured or explained. And yet that does not mean it doesn't exist."

"The sound that a heart makes, when it is breaking, is raw and ugly. And anguish, it's a waterfall."

"Could love be not grand gestures or empty vows, not promises meant to be broken, but instead a paper trail of forgiveness? A line of crumbs made of memories, to lead you back to the person who was waiting?"

Chapter 43: Jenna

Jenna closes out the story by describing her visits with her mother and the new relationship she has with Alice. She visits Alice during the moments just before waking, which we have learned is the point where a person is most likely to accept and engage with the spirit world.

Analysis
Jenna and Alice seemed to have found peace and consolation in spite of what happened at the Sanctuary. They have found closure and can now move on with their lives in a healthier manner.

Important Terms

Bearing witness
Elephant Whisperer

Study Questions

How does Jenna describe the elephant's grieving process?

How does that differ from what Alice had observed?

What does she suggest about a person or elephant's ability to know about someone's death? Is it believable that an elephant has thoughts in the same way that a human does?

Quotations

"If you think about someone you've loved and lost, you are already with them. The rest is just details."

Critical Reviews

Reviews ranged from 5 stars to 1 star. Out of 1,889 reviews on Amazon.com, 1,189 were 5 stars. Most five star reviews loved the elephant story-line and were intrigued by the character development and surprise ending. Although the main topic is about elephants, Picoult still gave impressed readers the dramatic investigation and intrigue they look for in Picoult's books.

Reviewers who gave her 3 stars or less seemed to have been fans of her previous work, but found this book boring with a tendency to repeat the so-called formulaic nature of her style.

Those who gave her 1 star tended to believe that she provided far too much detail about elephant life than was necessary to tell this story. Readers also disliked the surprise ending. They did not believe that the ending was worthwhile and felt that they could have spent their time reading another novel.

Final Thoughts

I can appreciate Picoult's trademark style of storytelling, but with the activist twist. She uses different characters to offer unique perspectives on difficult lives of elephants today. Elephants are becoming endangered and Picoult has deliberately brought her star power to address the massacre of elephants. This was an enjoyable read and I know that I have learned something new about the plight of elephants.

Glossary

Abject terror-*abject*: miserable or despicable; *terror*: intense fear

Alice-Jenna's mom and famous elephant researcher who disappears after the death of an employee which occurs at the Elephant Sanctuary.

Allomother-the *"it takes a village"* approach to elephant mothering that allows all females within the herd to care for a baby elephant; an individual other than the biological mother of an offspring that temporarily performs the functions of a mother.

Amnesiac-a person who loses a large block of interrelated memories

Amygdala-an almond-shaped part of the brain that is involved in the emotions of fear and aggression

Anecdotal evidence-Evidence that is collected based on personal observation, case studies, or random investigations rather than systematic scientific evaluation.

Anguish-excruciating or acute distress, suffering, or pain.

Anthropomorphic-ascribing human form or attributes to a being or thing that is not human

Apparated-to appear magically

Baptism-ceremonial immersion in water, or application of water; a trying or purifying experience or initiation

Bear witness-the act of being present, to personally see or perceive a thing; an eyewitness.

Behavior Modification-the direct changing of unwanted behavior by means of biofeedback or conditioning

Bioluminescensce-the production of light by living organisms

Catatonic-a physical state of having rigid muscles and mental stupor sometimes alternating between great excitement and confusion.

Chain of Evidence- is a series of events which, when viewed in sequence, account for the actions of a person during a particular period of time or the location of a piece of evidence during a specified time period.

Charlatan-a person who pretends to more knowledge or skill than he or she possesses.

Clairvoyance-the supernatural power of seeing objects or actions removed in space or time from natural viewing; quick intuitive knowledge of things and people.

Clairvoyant-a person having or claiming to have the power of seeing objects or actions beyond the range of natural vision.

Closure-bringing to an end or conclusion

Cognition-the act or process of knowing; perception

Cold reading-[in *Leaving Time*] psychically read someone without an appointment or previous introduction.

Collaring-to put a collar on.

Compartmentalize-to divide into categories or compartments

Culling-to choose, select or pick; to gather the choice things from.

De facto matriarch-matriarchy that exists in fact or in reality.

Death rituals-an established set of behavior or ceremony related to the death of an individual

Detritus-any disintegrated material; debris; waste

Electroluminescent-production of light by the flow of electrons

Elephant Advocate-a person who speaks or writes in support or defense of an elephant's cause

Elephant Graveyard-a burial site where elephants are buried after they die.

Elephant Whisperer-a person who has the unique ability to see the world through the eyes of an elephant.

Empathy-the intellectual identification with or vicarious experiencing of the feelings, thoughts, or attitudes of another.

En masse-in a mass; all together; as a group

Estrus Song-a song-like sound made during a period of maximum sexual receptivity of a female mammal indicating an interest in mating.

Ethereal-extremely delicate or refined; heavenly or celestial

Evolutionarily feasible-the process of change

Evolutionary advantage-the process of change in animal populations that function to its advantage

Extrapolate-to infer an unknown from something that is known

Extreme distress-the highest degree of pain, anxiety, or sorrow

Fantasy-imagination especially when extravagant and unrestrained; hallucination

Female in estrus-a female during a period of maximum sexual receptivity

Feral-existing in a natural state; not domesticated or cultivated; wild.

Fourth Dimension-a dimension beyond the kind of normal human experience that can be explained scientifically such as extra-sensory perception (ESP).

Free Contact- system which allows elephant keepers to share the same space with elephants while using a bullhook to hit, poke and intimidate the elephant as a means of control and domination.

Ghost-the soul of a dead person, a disembodied spirit imagined as wandering among or haunting living persons.

Gideon-an employee of the elephant sanctuary who is married to Grace and shares a special relationship with Alice

Grace-an employee of the elephant sanctuary who is married to Gideon

Grief-keen mental suffering or distress over a loss.

Hallucination-a sensory experience of something that does not exist outside the mind, caused by various physical and mental disorders

Heliotrope-a hairy plant that is cultivated for its small, fragrant purple flowers; any plant that turns towards the sun; a light tint of purple or reddish lavender.

Heroic courtesy-daring or noble polite behavior

Hippocampus- located in the brain, it plays important roles in the consolidation of information from short-term memory to long-term memory.

Hysterical strength-a show of force or power stemming from an uncontrollably emotional situation; irrational strength from fear or emotional shock

Implode-to burst inward

Indian Sari-a garment worn by Hindu women, consisting of a long piece of cotton or silk wrapped around the body with one end draped over the head or over one shoulder.

Institutionalize-to place or confine in an institution especially one for the care of mental illness or alcoholism.

Jenna-the persistent and intelligent daughter of two elephant advocates and researchers who is determined to investigate her mother's disappearance.

Kaleidoscope-a continually changing pattern of shapes and colors.

Kamba-an agricultural people of central Kenya renowned as traders and woodcarvers

Larynx-a structure in the throat area where a mammals vocal chords are located.

Leaving Time-phrase used by Jenna as a child when she referred to a nap.

Liar-person who tells lies

Mahout-the keeper or driver of an elephant

Manic or depressive episodes-(also called bipolar disorder) serious shifts in mood, energy, thinking, and behavior—from the highs of mania on one extreme, to the lows of depression on the other. Cycles may last for days, weeks, or months. The mood changes of bipolar disorder are so intense that they interfere with a person's ability to function.

Masai-an African people inhabiting the highlands of Kenya and Tanzania having a largely pastoral economy.

Mass burial site-a grave containing multiple number of human corpses, which may or may not be identified prior to burial.

Maura-an elephant, among many, who Alice can identify and sympathize with.

Melancholy-a gloomy state of mind especially when habitual or prolonged; depression

Memory-recalling or recognizing previous experiences

Metaphors-a figure of speech in which a word or phrase is applied to something else which is not literally applicable, but used in order to suggest a resemblance.

Metaphysical-concerned with abstract thought or subjects such as existence or truth; *archaic use,* imaginary or fanciful

Micromanage-to manage or control with excessive attention to minor details.

Migration-the process or act of moving or resettling from one place to another.

Mirror neurons- a neuron that fires both when an animal acts and when the animal observes the same action performed by another.

Molecular Consolidation Theory-a theory that suggests that a memory may be altered after it has been consolidated or processed by the brain.

Monsoon-the season during which the monsoon (heavy winds) blow, commonly marked by heavy rains; rainy season.

Murder-to kill or slaughter inhumanly or barbarously

Musth-a state or condition of violent, destructive frenzy occurring with the mating season in male elephants

Myths-any invented story, idea, or concept

Narcissism-excessive self-love; vanity

Negative reinforcement-an aversive stimulus being given and then retracted once the desired behavior as occurred (see also positive reinforcement)

Nevvie-an employee of the elephant sanctuary whose death at the elephant sanctuary remains a mystery

Nightmare-a terrifying dream in which a dreamer experiences feelings of helplessness, extreme anxiety or sorrow.

Open channeling-the act of receiving transmission and information from non-physical beings without any means of choosing to whom or how many beings you speak to.

Paranormal-of or related to the claimed occurrence of an event or perception that lacks scientific explanation

Pheromones-any chemical substance released by an animal that serves to influence the physiology or behavior of other members of the same species

Poacher-a person who trespasses on private property, especially to catch fish or game illegally.

Positive reinforcement-anything which, occurring in conjunction with an act, tends to increase the probability that the act will occur again.

Rage-violent anger

Reincarnation-the belief that the soul, upon death of the body, comes back to earth in another body or form.

Reverence-a feeling or attitude of deep respect or awe.

Sanctuary-a sacred or holy place; a tract of land where wildlife, especially those hunted for sport can breed and take refuge in safety from hunters.

Scrying-the practice of looking into a translucent ball or other material with the belief that things can be seen, such as spiritual visions.

Self-destruction-to destroy oneself

Serendipitously-found by accident; an aptitude for making desirable discoveries by accident.

Serenity-a psychic who is enlisted by Jenna to help her solve the mystery of her mother's disappearance

Sieve-an instrument with a mesh bottom used for separating coarse from fine parts of loose matter.

Skeptic-a person who questions the validity or authenticity of something purporting to be factual.

Somatic intuition-direct perception of truth felt in the body that is independent of any reasoning process

Spirits-a supernatural being without a body, especially one that inhabits a place or object or has a certain character (angel, demon, phantom)

Suicide-the intentional taking of one's own life.

Suspended Animation-a state of temporary cessation of necessary or vital functions.

Swamp witch-[in *Leaving Time]* searching for the truth without the use of psychic powers

Technicolor-flamboyant as in color, meaning or detail

Tether-a rope or chain by which an animal is tied to a fixed object to limit its range or movement.

Theory of mind-the ability to attribute mental states — beliefs, intents, desires, pretending, knowledge— to oneself and others and to understand that others have beliefs, desires, and intentions that are different from one's own.

Thomas-Jenna's dad who is institutionalized for mental health problems which become overwhelming after a series of events that occurs at the elephant sanctuary he owns and operates

Threshold-any place or point of entering or beginning; *psychology*, the point at which a stimulus is of sufficient intensity to produce an effect.

Trauma-an experience that produces psychological injury or pain.

Tsunami-an unusually large sea wave produced by an underwater volcanic eruption

Vicious cycle-a repeating situation or condition in which one problem causes another problem that makes the first problem worse.

Virgil-a detective enlisted by Jenna to help her solve the case of her mother's disappearance

Viscous sadness-sticky or thick unhappiness or grief

Water Poltergeist-a ghost or spirit supposed to manifest its presence by noises, knockings, or in this case, using water.

Recommended Reading

All citations were provided from the book itself. The following books have been recommended by Picoult herself:

Anthony, Lawrence. *The Elephant Whisperer*. Thomas Dunne Books, 2009.

Bradshaw, G. A. *Elephants on the Edge*. Yale University Press, 2009.

Coffey, Chip. *Growing Up Psychic*. Three Rivers Press, 2012.

Douglas-Hamilton, Iain, and Oria Douglas-Hamilton. *Among the Elephants*. Viking Press, 1975.

King, Barbara J. *How Animals Grieve*. University of Chicago Press, 2013.

Moss, Cynthia. Elephant Memories. William Morrow, 1988. Moss, Cynthia J., Harvey Croze, and Phyllis C. Lee, eds. *The Amboseli Elephants*. University of Chicago Press, 2011.

Masson, Jeffrey Moussaieff, and Susan McCarthy. *When Elephants Weep*. Delacorte Press, 1995.

O'Connell, Caitlin. *The Elephant's Secret Sense*. Free Press, 2007.

Poole, Joyce. *Coming of Age with Elephants*. Hyperion, 1996.

Sheldrick, Daphne. *Love, Life, and Elephants*. Farrar, Straus & Giroux, 2012.

Made in United States
Orlando, FL
10 December 2021

11461245R00052